HIS CURVY DESIRE

OBSESSED ALPHAS SERIES

JULIE SCARLET

CONTENTS

1

Mollie

I never get sick of the smell of cupcakes. I spend almost every day baking them, selling them, packing them up for delivery…and still that sweet, buttery smell makes my mouth water.

Not many people get to say they love their job, but I'm one of the lucky ones! I'm just finishing packing the rest of a huge order up — over two hundred cupcakes for a wedding.

We've only just managed to finish baking them on time.

I carefully arrange them into boxes of twelve, terrified that one wrong move could ruin them. It's like I'm playing a game of Operation. I move so slowly.

I can tell my tongue is sticking out, as it always does when I'm concentrating hard. The tip of my tongue is dry after what feels like hours of organising.

I can't help but admire the cakes. They have white frosting with gold flakes sprinkled on the top, finished off with little gold butterflies delicately balanced just slightly off-center.

They're going to look so gorgeous decorating the tables at the reception.

I mentally add the image to my list of ideas for my wedding plans, which is so far completely imaginary. I let out a little snort of laughter, a dangerous move as I'm positioning the last of the cakes in the final box. My hands shake a little as I snigger, but luckily there are no disasters.

I'm as single as can be and it's embarrassing to think I'm giving my wedding this much thought when there is a good chance that there will be no wedding at all.

My dating life isn't what I would call successful. The kind of guy I attract is completely the opposite of my type; I always seem to date the *nice* boys. I know that sounds a stupid thing to complain about, and I've only got myself to blame, really.

The blonde, bubbly (a nicer word than chubby) baker just sounds like the kind of girl that marries someone just as sweet as the cakes she makes. The truth is, a part of me – well, a *big* part of me- wants someone a little more complex than that - someone with a dark side, a tall, brooding, dominating character who can throw me around a room.

As IF HIS ears were burning, Max walks through the door. The chime of the bell as he opens the door snaps me out of my daydream. He's the owner - not just of the store, but the whole chain.

This is now an even worse time for me to be trying to carefully distribute the cakes into the box.

Every time I see him, my stomach flips, and my knees go weak. With his dark hair, his steely blue eyes, his chiseled jaw, it was like he was picked right out of a magazine.

He's quite a bit older than me, in his late thirties or early forties, I'd say. Little laughter lines are etched around the creases of his eyes, making them stand out even more.

His black hair is long and swept back off his face. There's always one disobedient curl that flops forward, and I always catch him absent-mindedly, trying to brush it away.

He's wearing a thin, black turtleneck jumper, which outlines the thickness of his arm muscles and the breadth of his shoulders.

His thick eyebrows always make him look like he's

deep in thought in the broody way that drives girls crazy.

I've been in love with Max since the moment I first saw him. I've been with the company for a few years now, and he still makes my heart somersault each time he makes a shop visit. I barely know him, not through any fault of his.

He's friendly enough – I've just never been able to hold any conversation with him without making a fool of myself. After a while, I stopped trying, instead avoiding any kind of social interaction with him out of the sheer terror that I would embarrass myself.

I realize how much I must have been staring, cupcake poised in my hand, looking like a moron, when his eyes meet mine.

His lips curl up into a subtle, crooked smile. I try to smile back, ignoring that my fair skin must be burning horrendously against my sandy hair.

My lips barely manage to move as I will myself to look normal. How difficult is it to smile?

"You finished yet, Mollie?" I turn sharply to see Gabby watching me with a knowing smirk on her face.

Her eyes twinkle mischievously to match her diamond ear stud, and she's lazily chewing gum with her mouth wide open.

We've been friends for a long time. I have never told her about my feelings for Max, but I never had to.

I'm as subtle as a fart in church, and she just loves to wind me up about him every time he comes into the store. It's probably easy for Gabby to think this is all fun and games. When it comes to guys, she has no trouble getting them.

Unlike me, Gabby's curves go in and out in all the right places, or perhaps the difference is that she has bits that actually go *in*. She knows just how to show them off as well.

For example, today, she's wearing a white shirt that's the tiniest bit too tight for her, exaggerating her perfect breasts.

She's also rolled her apron, so it's a little shorter, allowing her black jeans to show off her perfect bubble butt. She makes it look so effortless.

I would probably hate her if we weren't such good friends. Customers always love her and are naturally drawn to her, leaving me to remain invisible in the background.

"Just about," I said, trying my very best to sound totally relaxed by the company we now have in store. "I'm working on the last box." Gabby chuckles at my pathetic attempt to sound nonchalant.

Thankfully, she's a good enough friend not to wind me up anymore while Max is here, and goes back to wiping down the tables.

My mouth was bone dry as I try to ignore Max

walking slowly around the store. I keep my eyes glued to the floor and make my way over to the water machine.

It seems to take all my brainpower to remember all the various movements it takes to get there.

Left foot, right foot; raise a hand to pick up paper cup…what was *wrong* with me?

With a shaky hand, I pour water into the cup. I stay where I am to drink it, facing the machine, my back to the rest of the store. As I drink, I struggle to breathe at the same time.

My coordination has never been my strong suit, especially so when there's a hot guy around. I hover awkwardly with the cup pressed against my face, water slowly filling my parted lips as I try to remember how to breathe.

"Mollie?"

The voice comes from right behind. I don't even hear him sneak up. In shock, I spit vulgarly all down myself, water spraying all down my white shirt and hot pink apron.

I dare myself to look up at Max. His eyes are cold, but his mouth has a look of amusement on it. If the universe didn't hate me enough already, a cool breeze comes in through the window precisely at that same moment.

Embarrassment washes over me as I feel my

nipples harden instantly. There's no way they wouldn't be visible through this shirt! I want the ground to swallow me up. All I could do was hold his gaze, too frozen with humility for anything else.

"Why don't you clean yourself up and then see me in my office?"

He doesn't even wait for my response before turning on his heel and marching through the door behind the counter.

I turn to see Gabby looking at me with wide eyes that are silently saying, "Oh *shit!*"

The sinking feeling in my stomach still wasn't enough to distract me from how hot he looks, even from the back as he walks away.

I inhale the traces of his cologne that he's left behind, thankful he has his back to me and can't see me close my eyes as I take in his scent.

Am I about to be fired? The coldness in his voice must have meant that it couldn't have been anything good. I feel sick with nerves. He left the floor so quick that I got the impression he's in a hurry.

I better not dare waste his time by searching for a towel to sort myself out. As soon as my legs started to work again, although barely keeping me upright from the feeling of jelly between my hips and my ankles, I make my way into his office.

He's already behind the desk when I make my way

in. I carefully close the door behind me, already sensing Gabby straining to hear my bollocking.

When I eventually turn around to face him once again, I'm shocked to see his eyes are fixated on my soaking chest.

2

Max

I know she caught me staring at her chest. How
could I not? Seeing her nipples stand out
through the soaked fabric made me hard
instantly. I'm so thankful that I sat behind the desk so
she won't see anything.

God knows how she would react if she knew I was
hiding a throbbing erection from her. By the time I
come to my senses and shift my focus from her breasts
to her eyes, she's already looking at the ground, her
cheeks burning bright red in embarrassment.

It's turning me on, even more, to see her submis-
sively accepting me ogling her body, embarrassed
or not.

She doesn't cover herself up or storm out the room, furious with my perversion; instead, she just stands there and takes my leering, keeping her wet breasts in front of me to stare at.

Am I reading too much into this? Or is the real reason that she's so embarrassed her secret desire for me to stare at her body?

Mollie had always been hard to read; I had never been able to hold eye contact with her for longer than a few seconds. She has worked for my company for a few years now. I still remember the moment I first saw her like it was yesterday.

I came to the store on her first day. She had no idea I was the owner of the company, but even then seemed nervous as hell to talk to me.

She would laugh politely at my poor attempts at jokes, ask the normal questions, 'How's your day going?' 'Can I get you anything else?' but each time her eyes would quickly meet the floor once again.

The rare times our eyes would meet, however, there would be this electricity between us.

I felt the energy surge through my body. It was like the colors got a little brighter, and I would always feel this wave of both happiness and excitement wash over me, making my heart thump in my chest.

As quick as the moment would arrive, however, it would leave just as quickly. She would look away or walk off, and I would be left wondering if I had imagined the whole thing.

I think she's beautiful. Although I can't get her to relax around me, I can't help but watch how she is with other people.

It sounds creepy, I know, her smile beams across the room, and there will always be a few loose strands of golden blonde hair dancing across her face as she speaks in her exaggerated, animated kind of way.

She always wears bright colors; she literally lights up the room. Every time I see her chatting to a colleague or a customer, she is making them laugh or engaging in an excitable conversation. Only when it comes to me will she fall quiet, barely able to string a sentence together.

I think for most people this would have the opposite effect, but, to me, her nerves and sudden shyness turn me on even more. Although in the long run, I don't want her to be intimidated by me, it's hot as hell to know that I have that effect on her.

The problem is getting the chance to let her know how I feel without scaring her off completely. To be fair, staring at her tits probably did just the job…

"You haven't changed your clothes, Mollie?" I ask, trying to imply that the staring was only because I had noticed she was still in her wet clothes.

"I…er…I didn't want to keep you waiting." She

shivers slightly, the nerves probably running a chill through her. She bites her lip in uncertainty as she tries to work out if she has done the right thing or not.

She's driving me crazy, my bulge straining harder against my trousers. She holds her hands behind her back, as if not sure what to do with them, and it pushes her chest out even further.

All I can think about is grabbing the back of her hair and pulling her bitten lips and soaked breasts towards my aching cock…

"I'll keep this short. I don't want you getting cold." I see the side of her mouth twitched slightly into a smile, but her eyes remain glued to the floor.

"I'm opening a new store, over at Bridgeway. It's going to be our biggest branch yet. I want you to run it for me."

This time her head snaps up and her eyes met mine. There it is again, the heat, the flip in my stomach. Her eyes are a pale, perfect blue, with long lashes fluttering over her freckled nose.

"I…I'm flattered, Max!" I hadn't heard her say my name before. It sends a little shiver down my spine, especially the way she gasped it like that.

"But I couldn't accept such a huge offer. I'm not good enough, I would mess it up…" She looks back to the ground as if ashamed by her self-declared lack of capability.

A different kind of heat burns through me - a frustration that she can't understand how talented and capable she is.

"I want you to come to visit the store with me tomorrow."

"But I-"

"Mollie. I need someone who is capable and who I can trust to take on such a big project. I trust my own opinion, and you have been with us for years. We will visit the store tomorrow, and I'm sure you'll feel more comfortable once you see the place. But I don't want to hear any more about what you can and can't do, okay?"

She nods, biting her lip again. I love how she responds to my authoritative tone. No backchat, almost a little fearful. She has no idea how sexy she is.

"Good, I'll email you the address. I'll see you there at 10 am sharp."

She manages to whisper a quick thank you and goodbye before practically running out of the office.

I watch her go, her ass hypnotising me as it wiggles dramatically from side to side. I let out the grin I've been hiding from her as I think about having her all to myself tomorrow.

For all the years that I've known her, I've been dying to have proper time alone with her, but I've never been able to steal her for more than a few minutes.

Tomorrow will be different, and hopefully, my

patience will finally pay off so I can get to know the real Mollie.

patience will finally pay off so I can get to know the real Mollie.

3

Mollie

I'm pacing around my apartment like a woman possessed as I wait for my cab to arrive. I've already changed my outfit three times today, and I'm still not satisfied with my final choice.

Do I dress smartly and treat this as an interview? Do I wear more casual clothes and act aloof, and like I'm not remotely fazed by Max at all? Do I dare go dressed a little sexy and slutty?

I've decided on a white, capped sleeved blouse - with perhaps just one too many buttons undone- paired with a black pencil skirt to help suck me in and out at the right places and accentuate my curves.

I'm daring to wear little black heels, trying desperately to give my ass a bit of an extra boost, not that it needed any help on the size department.

I hardly ever wear heels, normally sticking to the comfort of sneakers or cute little pumps.

At least the obsessive pacing is helping me to practice tottering around in these heels without looking like a complete idiot.

I tactfully tie my hair back in a casual low ponytail to try and counterbalance the sexy outfit, so it doesn't look like I am trying too hard. I have a feeling Max will see straight through that, though.

At least if I have totally misread the signals he gave me yesterday in his office, I can make out like I was just trying to look professional.

The cab driver keeps trying to make light conversation on our journey, but I'm far too distracted. I mutter back one-word answers, but all I can think about is Max. My stomach is flipping with nerves.

I've loved him since the moment I met him, sure, but I haven't actually spent more than a few moments alone with him.

He makes me so nervous; how on earth am I going to pull this off without making a complete fool of myself?

He's waiting for me outside the restaurant when we pull up. He's wearing an outfit more casual than I've ever seen him in - normally at work, he's always so smartly dressed.

Today, he's wearing a red and black checkered shirt over a white top and black jeans. He looks so much younger, not that I mind him being an older guy.

I like the way his black curls are tinged with grey, and the slight lines etched around his eyes. But today, he's sporting a boyish, mischievous grin, and he seems to be standing taller, as if his shoulders aren't carrying as much weight.

He opens my cab door for me and holds out a hand to help me out. He even subtly hands the cab driver the fare. Could he be any more dreamy?

"Good morning, Mollie."

His voice is so silky. Hearing him say my name makes my knees go weak. I've always struggled to look him in the eye, but as he keeps hold of my hand, I can feel the heat between us.

I let myself get lost in his pale blue eyes, ignoring the fact that I must be grinning like an idiot.

"Hi," I just about managed to breathe. I see him eye my outfit up and down. Is it too much? Does he think I look like some kind of moron?

"You look great." I try to see a smirk or hint of a joke on his face, but there isn't one. In fact, he's looking at me with an expression that I don't recognise. His eyes are burning into me; it's making me feel hot under my clothes.

"I thought it would be a nice change from the apron." His greedy eyes soften, and he laughs lightly at my joke, immediately relaxing the heated atmosphere.

"Let me show you around."

The store is just gorgeous. The walls are mainly glass, so the sunlight pours through, and it's huge, definitely the biggest store I've ever worked in.

Every surface and piece of equipment is shiny and new, gleaming with lack of use. We don't speak as I take in space. I can feel him watching me as I walk around.

The light bounces from the surface to surface, and I felt so calm. I run my fingers along with the solid oak tables, feeling privileged that I'm probably one of the first to do so.

"Is there no one else here?" I expected there to be workmen or contractors of some kind, but it was just us.

"No…I wanted you to be the first to see it."

I looked at him, and he was watching me. Dare I say he looked nervous? I had never thought of Max being the kind of guy to get nervous, but his eyes were wide with anticipation of what I was going to say next.

I can feel the heat rising in my cheeks again. I need to change the topic before my cursed blushing clashed with my fair hair once again – it was not a good look. I scan my eyes around the room once again, picturing the bustle of customers and the wonderful smells that would come from this place.

"Does the kitchen have to stay here?" I ask, indicating to the far corner of the room. His eyes follow the direction I point in, but he looks back at me quizzically.

"It's just…there's an amazing view of the woodland over there, and the sunsets in that direction too. I think it would make an amazing view for customers to look at." He ponders my answer.

"And where would you put the kitchen?"

I consider his question for a few moments. "Over there," I point to the left corner by the entrance. "That only overlooks the parking lot, not to mention the amazing smells will filter right out into the street!"

His eyes flicker from corner to corner as he analyses my ideas. Did I speak out of turn? Is it rude to suggest what someone so successful does with their business? He lets out a sudden laugh.

"I'm sorry…I've insulted you."

"No!" he chuckles. He comes and stands right in front of me. "I'm just remembering you saying yesterday that you weren't good enough for this job?" I sigh in relief that he's not mad and let out a shy giggle myself.

"Ideas are one thing…executing them is another!" He opens his mouth to retaliate but decides against it.

Instead, he sighs and rests both of his hands on my shoulders. The heat coming from him makes me melt inside.

"You hungry?" he asks. I nod. "Let me take you to lunch, Mollie. We can talk more there."

4

Max

Spending time alone with Mollie is going so much better than I thought it would. I thought it would be nearly impossible to get anything out of her, just like it is at work, but she's already opening up to me.

Watching her mind wander as she walked around the store made me adore her even more, not to mention she looks hot as hell in her skirt and blouse. All I could think about was grabbing her and bending her over the counter.

My gut tells me she wouldn't be opposed to that idea, but I can't make my move just yet, not until I'm sure. I keep sneaking little side-glances at her as I drive us to the restaurant.

The way her tanned thighs are peaking out of her skirt is driving me crazy. Her blouse is *just* not see-through, or she's found the perfect matching bra to create the illusion that it is.

She catches me a few times, looking at her. We don't speak much, but we both let out a little childish laugh each time. I can't help but love that I still make her nervous after all these years.

We pull up at one of my favorite Mexican restaurants. She asks no questions about where we are or why I chose this place, and even follows blindly as I guide us to my table of choice by the window.

I love how trusting she is of me; no questions asked. Not only that, but it turns me on like hell to watch her do as she's told…

I ask a few questions about what she likes on the menu, and then I order for us both. Again, there's no protest. She smiles that big, beaming smile as I order, clearly happy with my choices for her.

We talk about the business of the new store. To my utter delight, she starts chatting away like a high school girl.

"I think milkshakes would sell really well too. Oh! And I've been reading up a lot of vegan recipes for cupcakes. I've made a few at home, and they're actually not that bad! I think there could be a huge market there, and in that store, we have the space to sell a much larger range…"

Her ideas are incredible, but seeing her look so passionate and excited is infectious. She looks so sure of herself like she can take over the world. *This* is the Mollie I knew was hiding from me, waiting for me to find her.

I listen and nod, but after a while, I wave her words away, and she immediately falls silent. Again… so obedient.

"Enough about work for now. I want to know about you, Mollie." She looks at me blankly. How can she still be so surprised that I'm showing interest in her?

"You want to know about me?"

"Yes, of course, I do. You've worked for me for years, and I know hardly anything about you. Did you grow up here?" She shakes her head.

"No, I moved here a few months before I started the job."

"With your family?"

"N-no." She looks down at her food. The atmosphere quickly changes.

"Is there something wrong?"

"No, no. It's just…my parents died in a car acci-dent. I moved here for a fresh start. It made it a little easier to move on, I guess. Does that sound awful? Like I'm trying to forget about them?"

I shake my head, knowing right there and then that I was so in love with her. "No," I sigh. "It doesn't sound awful at all. My Dad moved us here when my Mother died when I was a kid."

I can't say with any certainty who moved first, but within an instant, our hands met across the table as we silently realised that we both had gone through the same thing.

"Are you close? You and your Dad?"

"Not really. He's a businessman too, except he travels a lot. He's hardly ever home. It's been that way since we moved here."

"That must have been so hard for you."

I shrug, looking down at the table. "I guess now, it's fine. I've been raised to be fiercely independent and ambitious. I owe that to my Dad, I guess. I've had a pretty good life. But sure, as a kid, it wasn't the easiest time in the world." I'm playing it down massively.

It was a horrible, lonely childhood. I hadn't talked about it with anyone other than a therapist before, but something about Mollie just made everything want to come out. My thoughts, my feelings, my memories... everything I had ever kept hidden was now all rising to the surface.

She squeezes my hand again, but then instantly retracts it, as if suddenly realising what she was doing.

"*Anyway*," I try to say jokingly. "You going to run my store for me then?"

She laughs, loudly. It's such a wonderful sound.

"I still don't understand! Why me? I didn't even think you remembered me!"

"Oh, I remember you." She raises her eyebrow in a cheeky way, and I feel a twinge in my pants.

"I know what makes my business run well, and you have a keen eye for the operations of my stores. I need people I can trust."

"Is that so?" she asks, biting her lip. God, she's so sexy, and seeing this new mischievous side to her makes me even hornier. If she ends up needing to be put in her place, then I'll happily be the one to do it.

"Yes, that *is* so."

"You trust me?"

"Yes, I do. You're playing with your food, Mollie. Come on, eat up." She giggles again but does as she's told, sticking her tongue out before she takes a big mouthful. Oh, how badly I want to show her what happens to cheeky girls when they're mine…

I pay our bill, and we make our way towards my car. I'm not ready to see her go just yet.

"Have you got some time? We could stop by my place for a coffee and talk a little more. It's not far from here." I can see her eyes flicker with delight as she reads between the lines.

"To talk about the store a little more?" She asks, feigning innocence.

"Sure," I laugh, teasing her straight back. "What else?"

5

Mollie

My heart is beating a thousand times a minute as we drive to his house. I'm sure he can hear it hammering in my chest. I stare out the window so he can't see the big stupid grin I can't help but wear, and I'm sitting on my hands so he won't see them shaking.

I'm so nervous but excited at the same time. For years, I've been head over heels for Max, and here I am getting driven to his place at his invite after a very flirty lunch. I can't remember the last time I was this turned on.

There's a deep pull inside my lower stomach, aching even more as I press my thighs together. The anticipation is making me so nervous, though. He can be so intimidating, and he has this way of making me desperate to please him.

It's so hot the way that he takes control, but it makes me nervous as hell to think about what he has in store for me. I'm worried now I've created the wrong impression - I acted all flirty and confident back in the restaurant. It felt great to tease him like that, but I didn't expect it to lead to anything!

Now I'm heading to his place after not having sex for literally months, and I need to go in there and act like I know what I'm doing.

Just relax, I repeat in my head. *He'll take control, just make him work for it a little!*

WE PULL OUTSIDE HIS HOUSE, and my mouth drops open. This place is *huge!*

"What the f-" He laughs quietly at my outburst. The house had its own drive about a quarter-mile long; and here I thought we were just on a random country road.

The house is three stories tall, with a grand archway over the front door. The windows are huge and wrap around the entire building. It looks like Max enjoys natural light just as much as I do. There's a huge balcony on the top floor, fit with sun chairs, a hot tub, and a barbeque.

As we step through the front door, I see through the back windows that a huge swimming pool sits in the beautiful garden, surrounded by hundreds of exotic plants. The sun is glittering off the water as it ripples slightly in the warm breeze. This place is an absolute paradise.

"Max This house is heaven!" I'm still looking round in awe, trying to take it all in. "How do you ever leave this place and venture out into the real world?"

He shrugs. "It's not quite the same when there isn't someone special to share it with." I saw the quickest flicker of sadness in his eyes, but it's quickly replaced by that mischievous grin I didn't know he had until today.

He walks towards me; the movement wafts the smell of his expensive cologne over me. I close my eyes for the briefest of moments to take it in, and feel him gently tuck a loose strand of my hair behind my ear.

The touch sets my skin on fire; my thighs feel like they could burst out from my tight skirt. I can feel how instantly wet he makes me.

With all previous nerves melted away in the fire that is my sexual desire, I reach up and cup his face. His cheek is so perfectly shaved it feels smooth in my hand.

He looks deep into my eyes, and I'm totally lost. It's like we're having a conversation without even speaking.

"I've always wanted you, Mollie," he whispers.

"Really?"

"Yes, really. You caught my eye the moment I first saw you."

I couldn't help but laugh a little in disbelief. This is the most gorgeous guy I've ever seen. He turns heads wherever he goes, although he doesn't seem to notice all the girls staring at him.

Everyone at work mentions how hot he is. And out of everyone he could choose, he wants me? It doesn't make sense.

"Well, you can have me. You've always had me."

I reach up to kiss him, but to my shock and horror, he pulls back slightly. I look at him quizzically as hot embarrassment floods my face.

"Just…before anything happens, Mollie. I need to know this is what you really want. I want you, more than anything, but I need to be sure you know that this has nothing to do with me offering that job to you. You've got that job because of your skills and experience, nothing else. This…now…it has to be because deep down, you really want this."

I stare at him in disbelief - has he really had no idea that I've been crazy about him ever since I met him? Has he mistaken my crippling shyness for cool distance and indifference?

"*Yes*, I want you, Max. I've always wanted you." He sighs and rests his hands on my shoulders.

"This isn't just about lust, Mollie. I…I'm in love with you. I always have been." My mouth falls open in shock.

"*Really?*" I feel the biggest grin stretch across my face. I feel my heart swell within my chest.

He shrugs in a sheepish manner. It's not often he looks shy like this! I take his hands off my shoulders and hold them in my own. "You really love me?" I ask, shaking my head in disbelief.

"From the moment I first saw you, yes." He looks deep into my eyes as he says the magic words. I'm numb with shock.

How can Max…*Max*…the hottest guy, with a huge business and this gorgeous house…the guy who can have any girl in the world…how can he choose little old me out of literally everyone else?

"I love you, too," I say. It feels bizarre saying out loud something I've kept secret for so long. I've always been so sure that my feelings for Max would be nothing but ridiculed, and certainly not reciprocated!

He smiles in relief, and I realise now he was nervous with anticipation for my response to his declaration of his love for me. Does he really have no idea that I've felt this way for years?

That my love for him was so transparent that my friends make fun of me because I turn into a clumsy idiot every time he's around? How can he even be unaware that anyone could fall in love with him so easily?

"Well …you hid that very well!" I say in a pathetic attempt to hide my nerves.

"As did you," he grins in response. Then he kisses me, and it's more than I could have ever imagined. I get goosebumps all over my body. His lips feel so warm and smooth against mine.

He wraps his arms around me as the kiss grows deeper, and his warmth allows me to melt into him. If he didn't have such a good grip on me, I think my knees would have given way, and I would have collapsed to the ground.

I'm totally lost in the moment. There's no space in my head to be confused and shocked about his revelation of his feelings for me. It's just him and I, entangled in each other's bodies.

6

Max

We kiss for an indeterminate amount of time. I've thought about this moment for so long, but I could never have predicted how natural it would feel.

I wrap both my hands around her hair in the heat of passion and pull her in closer, pressing my already rock hard cock up against her. She moans longingly into my mouth as she feels my hardness, and it makes me want her even more.

I run my hands up and down her body, resisting the urge to rip her clothes right off her then and there.

She reaches down and grabs my hard cock through my pants. She gasps and pulls away from our kiss.

"Max...it's *huge!*" She reaches to undo my zip hungrily, but I grab her wrist and twist it behind her back, my other hand around her hair once again. I press my forehead heavily against hers.

"You're mine, yes?"

She nods desperately.

"*Say it,* Mollie!"

"I'm yours...I'm yours!" The words send a shiver down my spine. I'm aching to taste her, to feel her, to see her writhe round in pleasure.

"I tell you when to grab my cock, then. Understand?"

"I understand." Her eyes are wide and wild, her pupils dilated, and her cheeks flushed. I *knew* she was naturally submissive; I knew she would love being told what to do. I let go of her hair and her wrist, and she lets her arms fall slowly by her side.

I start to walk around her slowly. She keeps her eyes fixated on the ground, just like she had done so many times in my office. Just like the good girl, I knew she was, she doesn't move. She doesn't reach for me or say a word. She patiently waits for my next move.

I'm behind her now. I slowly pull her hair tie out and let her golden hair fall loose down her back. I gently push it over her left shoulder to reveal her neck, and I plant tiny little kisses, starting from her jaw and working my way down to her shoulder.

Her head lolls to the side as she lets out little

moans. I reach around with my hands and start massaging her breasts. My hands can barely cover them as I toy with the lace around the cups on her bra. She sticks her chest out in response, backing her ass up onto my hard cock.

"You have no idea how hard you're going to cum," I whisper in her ear. I feel her whole body shudder as she backs further into me, letting out a low whimper. I start to undo her blouse buttons one by one, ever so slowly. She reaches and starts helping with the buttons from the bottom of her blouse. I slap her hands away.

"Be patient, Mollie," I breathe into her ear. "I want to be the one who gets you naked." Her knees buck a little, and I squeeze her tightly to help her keep her balance.

Seeing how powerlessly horny she is makes my cock ache even more. I can't wait to sink it inside her wet lips, but I'm enjoying teasing her far too much.

I finish with the blouse and let it fall to the floor. She's wearing a black lacey bra, the kind that is only worn for sex.

"I think someone was anticipating getting fucked today, hmm?" She giggles softly. I give her a hard smack on the ass, and she jumps upright in shock.

"Mollie, did you know you were going to get fucked today?"

"I...I had hoped, but I wasn't sure..." I laugh loudly and smack her ass again.

"You're a good girl for preparing for it. Now let's see if the panties match the bra." I reach for the zip at her hip and pull it down. This time, she knows not to help but instead to wait patiently. I slide the skirt down her thick thighs to reveal a perfectly matching pair of black lacey panties.

"Such a good girl," I mutter as she steps out of the skirt. There's a counter just in front of her, and I gently lean her forward to indicate her to place her hands on the surface. I step back to admire the view as she's bent over in her sexy, matching underwear.

She waits patiently for my next move, and I'm desperate to continue, but it's so hot watching her wait so obediently for me. She doesn't even look around to check what I'm doing or where I am, she just waits; her hands spread on the counter, her head bent forward in submission.

"Spread your legs a little, Mollie." She does so without a moment's hesitation. Her huge thighs now have a small gap between them, and it's all the space I need. I reach forward and slide two fingers between her thighs.

She moans loudly, and I'm thrilled to feel how soaked her panties are against my fingers. I rub against the fabric slowly, reveling in the sound of her moans and pants.

After a little while, I tuck my fingers under the fabric to feel her wet slit. Her whole body convulses, but still, she doesn't remove her hands from the counter, just balling them up into fists.

I let a smirk spread across my face as I feel the control I have over her body. My finger quickly finds her swollen clit, and I ever so gently start to rub. She is so patient as I toy with her, even though I can see how desperate she is to cum.

I could spend all day doing this, teasing her to orgasm. Her muffled cries tell me she's biting hard down on her lip.

We're interrupted loudly by my cell phone ringing. I want more than anything just to ignore it and carry on, but my gut tells me it's something important.

"Wait there, baby." I take my phone out of my pocket and go into the next room to answer it. I look back round just before I'm there and see to my delight she is still bent over the counter, just as I requested.

7

———

Mollie

He comes storming back into the room. I can already feel that the atmosphere has changed and I stand up, covering myself slightly.

"Mollie, I'm so sorry. It's work. Something's… happened. There's been a fire at one of the stores. I need to get straight there. I'll call you a cab…we'll pick up where we left off another time."

He barely looks at me as he gathers my clothes up off the floor and practically throws them in my direction. He's running around manically, grabbing keys and his wallet, talking on the phone to a cab company for me.

All of a sudden, I feel humiliated to be standing there in my underwear in the middle of his front room. How can a vibe change so quickly? He looks over at me in a kind of impatient way, and I clumsily start to put my clothes back on.

My hands are shaking with him making me feel so rushed, not to mention being that close to orgasm doesn't exactly make you feel that steady to begin with. I desperately try to blink back hot tears as embarrassment washes over me.

When I've dressed again, which feels like an eternity after fumbling with my buttons in such an awkward atmosphere, he opens the front door, pretty much insinuating for me to get the hell out.

"The cab will be here in a few minutes," he says as he ushers us both out of the door, slamming it shut behind him. He kissed me on the forehead for the briefest of moments before jumping into his car.

"I promise I'll be in touch as soon as this is sorted," he calls down from the window. "I'm sorry, I just have to go and get this sorted."

Then he drives off, leaving me outside his house. I touch my forehead lightly, where he just kissed me. What the hell just happened? I get that he had an emergency, but how can he just switch off like that?

I try not to get upset, telling myself that he'll call later than day, maybe even take me to a nice dinner to make up for it. We would laugh at how random it was and put the whole thing behind us.

Then he would take me home, and we'd finish what we started…

BUT ALMOST A WEEK PASSES, and I hear nothing from Max. I don't see him around any of the offices, and he doesn't call or text. I do hear about the fire at one of the stores downtown, not that I doubted the truth of it, but I still don't understand how it could make him act like he's forgotten what happened between us.

The past few nights, I've been crying myself to sleep, convinced that I imagined the whole thing, or that it was just him saying whatever he had to get me naked.

I'm so angry with myself for being such a gullible idiot. As if the hot boss wants me the way he says he did.

It's not hard to tell when something is on my mind. I'm normally so happy and excitable (probably to an annoying level) that it's obvious when I'm upset. Gabby notices it straight away.

"Will you *please* tell me what's wrong, Mollie?" We're cleaning down at the end of a shift. She'd been pestering me all day, asking what's wrong.

She's my friend, and she's worried, but I can't risk

anyone in the company finding out about Max. Gabby is a good friend, but she's one hell of a gossip.

If I told her truth, the whole company would know by the end of the day. I couldn't handle that level of humiliation.

"It's just…guy trouble." I say with my back to her, wiping down the tables.

"Oh?"

"It's nothing."

"I didn't know you were seeing anyone."

"Well, everything happened really fast. It was early days, and I didn't think it was worth mentioning anyway. I wouldn't even say I had been 'seeing anyone.'"

I turn around, and she has stopped working, her arms folded across her chest. Her eyes are narrowed; she's not used to me being this secretive with her.

I need to say something, or she'll just keep going. I take a minute to think tactfully about what to say.

"There's this guy…He said all these things about how he's always wanted me and made me feel so good about myself. He even told me he loved me and had done for years!

Things happened at his place, but he practically ran off with this emergency, and I haven't heard from him since last week."

"Oh honey," Gabby says as she carries on cleaning the coffee machine. "Guys can be such assholes. They say whatever they have to say to get us into bed. They're shameless! Don't feel bad, Mollie. It's happened to all of us!"

"It just doesn't seem like him. I don't understand…"

"I'm telling you, guys become Oscar-winning actors when they want to get laid! Don't waste any more of your time on him, Mollie. Trust me."

"But I really felt like there was this…I don't know… *connection* between us. It was like this unspoken understanding. I already made it very clear I was going to sleep with him, but even then, he made an effort to tell me he loved me. Why would he do that if it wasn't true?"

"Oh, Mollie…" Gabby is avoiding looking me in the eye as she cleans more frantically. Her sympathetic tone makes me flush with embarrassment.

"Some guys just like to mess with a girl's head. It's sick, honestly. I'm so sorry, honey. I think some guys can even believe they are in love when they're horny enough, it's just something their dicks tell them to try and successfully get a girl into bed. You're not alone, though, sweetie, the amount of stories I hear about girls thinking everything is going well with a guy only to find out he's disappeared into thin air is unbelievable!"

I feel my cheeks burn with humiliation. Of course, she's right. Why would the super hot millionaire bachelor waste his time falling in love with a shy, fat girl like me?

I end the conversation there to avoid bursting into tears, and soon enough, we lock up the store, and I head home. As soon as I'm alone, the tears start pouring once again. It just doesn't make sense.

Did I imagine the whole thing? Did the fact that I've been in love with Max for years mean the tiniest indication that he felt the same way made me believe him like an idiot?

I'm haunted by images in my head of him laughing with his friends, telling them the story of how easily he got the chubby girl into bed by pretending there was a big job offer and that he loved her. I imagine them all roaring their heads off in laughter, and I feel even more like an idiot.

There's a knock on the door. I ignore it – I'm not in the mood for whoever is on the other side. Whether it's a friend, a salesperson, or a Jehovah's Witness, they can all wait; I just want to wallow in my self-pity for now.

The knocking comes again, and again. I sigh loudly as I realise there aren't going away of their own accord and storm to the door full of rage, ready to tell whoever it is to piss off and slam the door in their face.

I open the door.

It's Max.

8

Max

I almost take a step back when she answers the door. She looks furious. Her expression quickly changes from anger to shock when she sees me.

Her eyes are red and blotchy, and I feel a sense of shame wash over me, as I know I'm the one that's caused her pain.

"What are you-?"

"I've come to explain," I brandish a bunch of pink roses from behind my back, "and to apologise."

She hesitates for a moment, clearly unsure what to say or do next. Her mouth flickers a little into a smile as she sees the flowers, but her eyes are eyeing me up, skeptical of my intentions.

"They're your favourite, aren't they?" I had heard her talking about them before with a customer, months ago.

I remember making a mental note in case I ever had the opportunity to buy flowers for her, although in all the hypothetical scenarios in my head, I was always giving her flowers for good reasons, not because I was in the doghouse.

She nods slowly, narrowing her eyes in confusion as she silently recalls that she and I have never discussed her favorite flowers before.

"I don't know whether to be happy, angry, or creeped out that you know that." Her voice is so unnaturally curt that it cuts right through me. I hang my head in shame. I had no intention of messing with her head like this.

"May I come in?" I ask, when the tension gets too much to bear. "I really just want a chance to explain and apologize. After that, if you don't want to hear from me again, then I will totally respect that and leave you alone."

She waits for another few painfully long moments. "Um...yeah, I guess," she says eventually. She steps back and lets me into her apartment. I step through into the quaint little bungalow.

There's color everywhere; the cushions on the couch, the various indoor plants dotted all the way around the room, blankets, ornaments. It's like a rainbow exploded in here. It's so perfectly Mollie that I can't help but smile as I look around, t

hat is until I look back at her and see she's looking angry once again. Her arms are folded over her chest, defensively. I gently place the flowers down on the coffee table.

"I'm sorry I haven't been in touch, Mollie." She rolls her eyes at me. In another scenario, that would turn me on so much. That kind of cheek doesn't normally fly, but I easily suppress my arousal, seeing her so upset.

"It's been a nightmare sorting out the store since the fire. The insurance paperwork…my head's been all over the place. I kept meaning to call you-"

"But, you didn't."

"No, I didn't. Every time I went to, something else came up that I had to deal with. It's been a crazy week, and I just kept losing track of time. It's no excuse, really. I'm just so sorry, and I want to make it up to you."

She starts pacing, scratching her head as if she's trying to work something out.

"I don't understand!" she says, throwing her hands up into the air, exasperated. "I can't tell if this is just more bullshit to try and get me back into bed. I can't tell if you're a fantastic liar or just an idiot that should have thought about calling or dropping a text before disappearing for a week."

"Mollie," I step towards her, reaching up to place my hands on her shoulders. "I promise you it's the latter. I'm a complete and utter idiot." She bats my hands away with a hard smack.

"*Don't.* I'm trying to think. I can't work you out. How do I know you're not just taking advantage of me? How do I know that you won't just disappear again if I forgive you today?"

"Because I'm in love with you."

A silence falls heavily upon us. After what feels like an eternity, she starts shaking her head, covering her ears with her hands like a child.

"Don't say that. You don't mean that. You're just saying what I want to hear."

"I'm not, Mollie. I've been in love with you ever since I first laid eyes on you." She's still walking around like a madwoman as if trying to shake the words out of her head.

"No, you don't. You're just- you're just-" I grab her and twist her round to face me, pushing her back against the wall behind her. I pull her wrists from her ears and place them high above her head.

It all happens so fast - I'm petrified I'm going to lose her. I need to make her see the truth.

"I *do* love you, Mollie! And you love me, too, don't you?" She wriggles slightly against me as I restrain her, but I squeeze her wrists harder. I move them both into one hand and use my free one to grab her chin and pull her face towards mine.

"I love you, do you understand me? If I have to spend every day proving that to you, then so be it. I'd like to start with today." I lean forward and kiss her deeply.

Thankfully, after a stunned moment, she returns the kiss. It's passionate and hot; I can feel her whole body relaxing into me.

I pull away when I feel her tears rub off onto my cheek. I relax my hold on her and let her arms fall back to her side.

"You're still upset with me?" I say as I wipe her tears away with the sleeve of my shirt.

"No," she laughed and sobbed at the same time. "They're happy tears, I promise! I just never thought I would have this with anyone. Since my family is gone, I've been so scared to love again. I just…I thought you were gone too."

I pull her into a tight hug. She laughs off the rest of her tears, and soon we are kissing again. They start off slow and romantic, but the heat soon builds between us, and our breaths become more ragged as our hands frantically grab at each other.

My hands are grabbing her ass, and hers are in my hair.

"I believe I owe you an orgasm?" I whisper in her ear. She moans loudly in response. I look around the room, deciding where I want her. "I want you on the couch." I step back slightly. "But first, I want to watch you take off your clothes."

She starts pulling off her shirt, and I see her eyeing the bulge in my pants greedily. "Don't worry," I say, reading her mind. "You'll be seeing my cock soon enough, but I'm going to make you cum hard before I even get naked."

9

Mollie

I would never normally dream of just stripping down like this; I usually prefer taking my clothes off under sheets in the dark. But the way Max was looking at me makes me feel like a goddess. I feel so sexy watching him eyeing me up hungrily.

I pull off my shirt and pants, slowing things down as I get down to just my underwear. I take my bra off strap by strap before carefully removing it from my breasts.

Then I turn around to take off my panties so that my ass is bent over in front of him. He smacks me on the ass hard as my panties reach my ankles, and I let out a loud moan.

"On the couch. Now."

I do as I'm told. Anticipation turns my legs to jelly, and I'm soaking wet between my thighs. My ass cheek tingles playfully from the spank. I turn to face him as I reach the couch.

His eyes are fixated on me. He looks so *serious* - his jaw is set, and his eyes are gleaming. He pulls off his shirt. His body is just as I imagined it, sculpted to perfection, and his muscles cast little shadows all over his chest and arms.

A neat trail of hair leads from his belly button down under his pants, drawing my attention to the huge bulge straining against the fabric.

"Sit."

I sit in the middle of the couch. He gets onto his knees and pushes my knees apart, exposing me. The fire in my pussy is burning now as he licks his lips with the wet tongue I know is about to touch me.

My hands find their way into his hair, trying to guide him towards me subtly. He grins, probably sensing my desperation. Instead, he kisses my right knee lightly and then starts to plant a tiny little kiss in a path leading up my thigh.

He's going so slowly, obviously enjoying driving me crazy. Each kiss sends waves of heat through my body, pulling harder on the ache in my lower stomach. I wriggle my body, sensitive to his touch.

He wraps his arms firmly around each of my legs

to keep me in place. He gets closer and closer to my pussy, but just as I think my relief is going to come, he skips right over. He's so close I can feel his breath on my clit.

Less than a moment later, he's on my left leg, working his kisses back down to my knee.

"Please," is just about all I can whisper. My breaths are the tiniest little gasps as the anticipation builds. I feel him laugh softly, almost sinisterly. He clearly loves having this hold over me.

"Say you're mine," he commands.

"I'm yours, I promise. I love you. *Please*, Max." My words sound like the ramblings of a madwoman. He grins, clearly satisfied with my answer, and finally lets his tongue reach my sweet spot.

I let out a loud cry in a release. He moves his tongue around my clit in a perfect rhythm, alternating between slow and fast movements to keep me on my toes.

As he senses I'm close, which doesn't take long at all, he slides two fingers into my slit, still stimulating me with his tongue. I feel him hook his fingers within me, pushing my clit forward from behind.

His fingers and tongue work in perfect unison, and within minutes I'm screaming his name and moaning hard as I implode, cumming hard.

He doesn't stop, letting me ride out my orgasm in slow waves. It seems to last for longer than any other

I've known. Every time I think it's over and I start to come back down to earth, he moves his tongue once again or strokes me inside, and I feel my body shudder.

When I eventually open my eyes, I see Max has gotten to his feet. To my delight, he's unbuttoning his pants. He frees his cock from his pants and underwear.

It's so rock hard and big that I let out a shocked gasp. The bulge in his pants did *not* do justice for the beast that was hanging in front of me. He grabs his cock roughly, watching me intently.

"You want this, don't you?" I nod frantically, unable to get my words out.

"Then go lie on your bed, face down on all fours." He helps me to my feet, steadying me as my legs threaten to give way. He then waits as I make my way to the bedroom. I don't hear him follow me, but I know not to turn around or call for him.

I pull all the blankets off my bed and do as I was told. I bury my face into one of my pillows and eagerly wait for him in doggy position, my soaked pussy facing the direction of the door. It feels like the longest time before I hear him come through the door.

Even then, I feel him move around the bed, pacing slowly to keep me on my toes. I know he's testing me, but I don't say anything or move from my position.

He starts to run his hands up and down my back and over my ass as he takes his slow steps around the room. I still don't move, only letting out little moans to show my eagerness.

After what feels like an eternity, I feel him climb onto the bed from behind. He strokes his hard cock along the opening of my pussy and spanks me again on the ass. My whole body bucks in response; I feel both exhausted and exhilarated all at the same time.

"Please…please fuck me, Max." I pant. "I need your cock." He laughs softly. It amazes me and turns me on so much that he can stay in control like that, unlike myself, who's a quivering wreck driven mad with arousal.

He reaches over me from behind to lightly kiss me on the neck, pressing his erection up against me. As soon as he straightens up again, he sinks it into me. I moan deeply as I feel myself stretch around his monstrous length.

He starts slow, making sure I can take all of him, and then once satisfied my body has adjusted to him, he speeds up. Harder and faster, he thrusts into me, and each time sends more waves of pleasure through me.

10

Max.

Her screams of pleasure are enough to make me want to cum there and then, not to mention watching her huge, gorgeous ass bouncing around as I keep pumping away at her.

Her cheeks have little pink marks from where I've spanked her. The rhythm was hypnotic, but I get to a point where I want to see her face again.

I want to see her contort in pleasure, and look deep into her eyes as I claim her as mine.

"Turn over," I whisper in her ear before pulling out. She does so instantly, waiting for my next direction on her back with her legs spread. I'm done with teasing; I've gotten myself too worked up to be able to wait anymore.

I guide my cock into her once again, leaning forward to grab her breasts. I pinch her nipples and massage her breasts as I keep thrusting. I can't take my eyes off her; her lips keep alternating between hanging in a slack 'o' shape and being bitten down hard as the pleasure washes over her.

When her eyes aren't closed as she gets lost in the moment, she's looking deep into my eyes. It's like we're having a conversation without even speaking. All of a sudden, she grins up at me, and I can't help but return the gesture. I kiss her, hard, and she kisses me back.

Sweat starts to form on my forehead as I continue to fuck her, but the adrenaline makes me harder still. As we continue to kiss, I hear a low moan start to rise from her throat.

She's close to cumming again, starting to writhe in pleasure. I'm close myself, and her noises are just making me even hornier.

"Come on, baby, cum again for me." As I thrust as hard as I can, I move one hand down to her clit, and the other around her throat to keep her in place so that the sensation is stronger.

Within moments, she's collapsing around me. She screams loudly, and watching her succumb is enough to tip me over the edge. I feel monumental wave of pleasure, and my hot cum shoots deep inside of her.

We're both muttering unintelligibly, holding on to each tightly. Our mouths find each other in the chaos of our entangled bodies, and we kiss between ragged breaths.

As the power of our orgasms start to subside, our other senses come back to life. I open my eyes, and she's already looking into them.

"I love you," she breathes. Her hair is all over the place, sweat making it stick to her forehead, I brush it gently out of the way and tuck it behind her ear. Here, now, in this moment — she has never looked so beautiful.

"I love you, too, Mollie. I always have."

EPILOGUE

Mollie

It's a year later - the best year of my life, in fact. I wake up in Max's bed – well, *our* bed. We opened the new store together, and he's left me to run it while he carries on looking after the empire.

It's the perfect match. We get to see each other all the time, but I can still say with confidence that I'm managing a store all by myself, just like I have always dreamed.

I didn't realize I had woken up to the sound of Max's footsteps coming up the stairs. Like the mind reader he is, he comes bearing two cups of coffee, hot steam still billowing out from beneath the lids.

"Mmm," I say as I lazily start to sit up, gratefully

taking my cup from his hands. Surprisingly, he sets his cup down and leaves the room again. I listen carefully, trying to figure out if something is wrong or not.

"Max?" I call out into the hallway from the bed. "Are you okay?" I hear no response from him, but I can hear his footsteps shuffling around on the downstairs floor, so he must be able to hear me.

"Max?"

"I'm fine!" he shouts up the stairs. His breath sounds ragged like he's wrestling someone.

"Is something wrong?"

"No! No. Stay there. I'm coming back up."

It was, in fact, the complete opposite of wrong; Max comes back into the room, this time carrying the tiniest puppy. A golden retriever, with a huge red bow tied around his collar.

The puppy is wriggling wildly with excitement. Max was barely able to contain him in his arms, which explains the panting I could hear from downstairs.

"Oh my god, Max! Who is *this?*" I take the puppy from his outstretched hands and hold him closer to my chest, my heart already about to explode with love.

The puppy instantly calms down and nuzzles himself deeply into my chest, making the kind of adorable squeaks that could break anyone's heart. Max laughs loudly.

"He's been going nuts the whole time I've had him. I've barely been to keep him still, it took me ages to get the bow attached to him! He takes one look at you and instantly feels relaxed. Why am I not surprised?" I look up, and he winks at me.

"I guess I can tame even the wildest of beasts," I say, in a poor attempt at sounding sexy and seductive. He laughs again and kisses me on my shoulder.

"Happy anniversary, Mollie." His kisses carry on from my shoulder and reach up to my cheek. I giggle as the sensation feels good and ticklish at the same time, sending little shockwaves up my skin.

"And here I was, thinking you had forgotten it was our anniversary!" It was true. There had been no mention of our anniversary all month. I remembered the day he told me he loved and stood outside with pink roses begging for my forgiveness like it was yesterday.

But I had thought it was just me being a loser to commit the date to memory, like some obsessive teen who held sentimental value in the smallest of things.

That was why I didn't mention anything. Perhaps there will always be a small part of me that worries Max will wake up and realize he could do so much better than someone like me, the chubby loser who's been infatuated with him for years.

Max sits beside me on the bed, running his hand up and down my silk pajamas. He always likes to dress me in the finest things, making me feel like a princess.

"As if I could forget the day my life started." He says the words so quietly I almost didn't hear him.

"Oh, Max!"

"I mean it, Mollie. This has, without a doubt, been the happiest year of my life, and it's all thanks to you." A lump quickly forms in my throat. It's true; we've been unbelievably happy. I never thought this was possible for someone like me.

"Marry me, Mollie."

I hadn't even realized he had slid off the bed and gotten down on to one knee. He's holding an enormous ring in his hands.

"Max! Are you serious? You really mean it?"

"Oh, I'm serious, baby. More than I've ever been. So, will you? Marry me?"

As if he even needs to ask. "*Yes!*" I squeal. "Of course I'll marry you!" If I weren't holding the puppy, I would have thrown myself at him in my excitement. Instead, I hold out my hand to him, my fingers shaking with emotion. He tenderly holds me and slides the ring onto my finger. It's a perfect fit.

He reaches over and strokes the puppy as he nestles himself in my arms. I feel like I'm about to burst into tears I'm so happy. Max can see this in my eye and leans over to kiss me deeply. Here on this bed is my family, and it just got a little bigger.

"Who would have thought a year ago that this is where we would be?"

I set the puppy down on the floor so he can explore his new home. I thank Max over and over as I pull him closer to me.

"Now, here's *your* anniversary present," I giggle as I clumsily remove my pajamas. Max sighs in satisfaction and pulls off his pants.

We kiss, and we hold each other for a little while first, basking in the pure happiness that we're so lucky to have.

The End

My book "His Curvy Prize" is available exclusively for my email subscribers. It is a romance between older Tattoo artist and a younger curvy girl. Their love starts from a Revenge! Want to read it?

Subscribe to newsletter and receive my book for FREE!

ALSO BY JULIE SCARLET

ABOUT THE AUTHOR

Julie Scarlet loves writing about hot, possessive alphas and sweet, independent woman. All her books are steamy with ice-melting hot scenes. There is always a guaranteed happy ending. Check out her books on Amazon that set you on fire!